10667516

THE
DINOSAURS
NEXT DOOR

Harriet Castor
Adapted by Lesley Sims

Illustrated by Teri Gower

Reading Consultant: Alison Kelly
Roehampton University of Surrey

Contents

Chapter 1 Mr. Puff   3

Chapter 2 The eggs   7

Chapter 3 Bigger and bigger   18

Chapter 4 KABOOM!   24

Chapter 5 Shrunk   31

Chapter 6 Cat to the rescue   39

Mr. Puff

Mr. Puff lived in a tall, blue house. Outside, it looked a little odd. Inside, it was even stranger.

Mr. Puff was an inventor.
His whole house was
crammed with amazing
inventions.

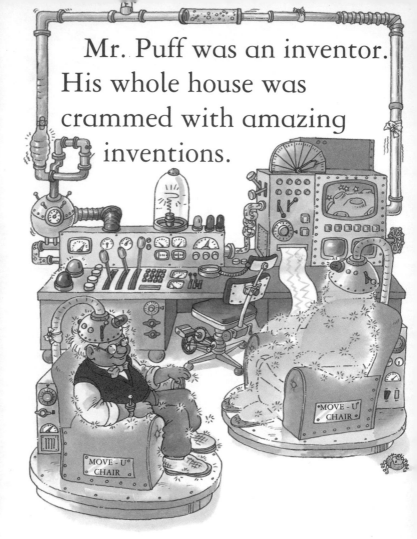

His latest invention moved
him from place to place in
an instant.

Before that, he invented a robot to clean up spills.

And before that, he invented the Wheelie Cup. (But it spilled most of his tea, which was why he invented the robot.)

His new project wasn't an invention at all. But it was so exciting he had asked Sam, his friend from next door, to see it.

Sam had promised to come over after school.

Chapter 2

The eggs

When Sam arrived, Mr. Puff was bursting with excitement.

He led Sam to his study and dived under a table.

They have to be kept in the dark until the last moment...

With a smile, Mr. Puff came out with a basket.

"Eggs?" said Sam, looking at the four big eggs.

"These aren't just any old eggs," said Mr. Puff. "They're...

...dinosaur eggs!"

"What?" cried Sam. "But dinosaurs died out zillions of years ago. How...? Where...?"

Mr. Puff looked mysterious. "Oh, they were to pay me for an invention," he said.

Just then, the blue spotted egg began to jiggle and jump and bump in the basket.

A crack
appeared,
zigzagging
along
the shell...

...then another...
...and another...

...until finally,
a little
green head
burst out.
"Wow!"
said Sam.

The creature stared at Sam. Sam stared back.

"Isn't it wonderful?" said Mr. Puff.

It's unbelievable! It's fantastic!

"But is it a dinosaur?" said Sam. Was it possible? It did look like a dinosaur.

As they watched, the other eggs began to jiggle and jump and bump in the basket.

Their shells shattered. The eggs had hatched.

The baby dinosaurs were very lively. They looked around, making excited squeaks.

"I expect they're hungry," said Mr. Puff.

"Let me go home for my dinosaur book!" said Sam and raced off. Soon, he was back.

"That one looks like ours!" said Sam. He pointed to a blue dinosaur with red spikes on its head.

"That one eats meat then," said Mr. Puff. "But some dinosaurs only eat plants."

They weren't sure what sort of dinosaurs the others were.

So Sam put out a large plate of cat food and a large plate of salad, just in case.

"It's my dinnertime too," said Sam. "I have to go. But I'll be back. I must be the only person with dinosaurs next door!"

Chapter 3

Bigger and bigger

Over the next three days,
Mr. Puff watched the
dinosaurs. He watched
them grow... and grow...

...and grow.
  By day four, he had to
invent an extra-long ruler
to measure them all.

By the fifth day, he was worried.

They're getting fierce.

"They just keep growing!"
he told Sam.

"Can't you invent something
to stop them?" Sam asked.

"That's it!" cried Mr. Puff.
He ran up to his dark, dusty
attic...

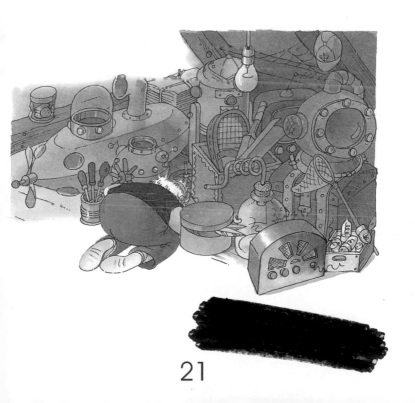

...and came back with a silver
box on wheels. A yellow hose
sat coiled like a snake on top.
"What is it?" asked Sam.

22

"This is my Size-O-Machine," Mr. Puff said proudly. "It makes things shrink or grow."

"Perfect!" said Sam. "Does it work?"

"Of course it works!" said Mr. Puff. "Ready, steady, fire!"

Chapter 4

KABOOM!

"Oh dear!" said Mr. Puff.
"Something must be wrong."

He peered inside the machine. "Ah!" he said. "I had my wires crossed. Try now Sam."

Sam picked up the hose.

"Ready, steady, fire!" said Mr. Puff.

KABOOM!

The dinosaur vanished.
"Where has it gone?" asked
Mr. Puff. "Did I shrink it
too much?"

Sam looked down the hose.
"Careful!" said Mr. Puff. "I
don't want you shrinking too."

27

They shrank one dinosaur in the kitchen. Another was outside, having a snack.

"Ready, steady, fire!" said Mr. Puff.

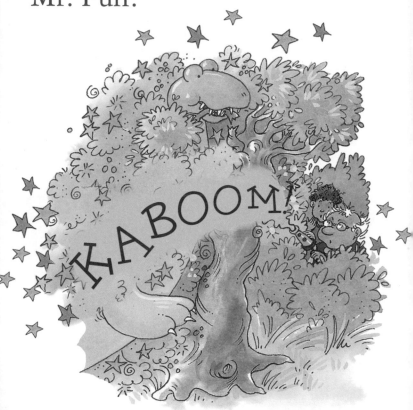

KABOOM!

But where was the last dinosaur? Just then, they heard a crash from the bathroom.

"Ready, steady, fire!" said
Mr. Puff.

But as Sam took aim, he
slipped. The hose flew from
his hands...

KABOOM!

Chapter 5

Shrunk

Fantastic! It works on people too!

Starry smoke filled the room. When it cleared, Sam was in shock. He was smaller than the bottle of bath oil.

"It's shrunk us as well as the dinosaur!" began Sam. He heard a roar behind him. "Run!"

Suddenly, the dinosaur looked at the door. Sam and Mr. Puff dived for cover.

The dinosaur should have hidden too.

Mr. Puff's cat was coming.
She took one look at the
dinosaur and chased it away.

"Quick!" said Mr. Puff.
"We must change to our
normal size before that
dinosaur comes back."

First, they had to move the
dial. Sam pushed. Mr. Puff
pulled. It was hard work.

Then they dragged the hose into place. By now, they were exhausted.

"Everything's hard when you're this small," Sam panted.

"Cheer up!" said Mr. Puff.
"We just have to turn it on."
But they couldn't shift
the lever.

"I hope we don't break it,"
said Sam. Mr. Puff didn't have
any puff to say anything. They
climbed off the machine. What
were they going to do?

Chapter 6

Cat to the rescue

Just then, the cat jumped
up onto the Size-O-Machine.
The lever moved.

KABOOM!

Clouds of smoke filled the room. Sam and Mr. Puff started to grow... and grow... and grow...

They were back to normal at last.

"Now, what are those dinosaurs up to?" said Mr. Puff.

The dinosaurs were running all over the house. Sam tried to help catch them.

The dinosaurs thought it was a game.

"Got you!" cried Mr. Puff as he scooped up the blue dinosaur.

"Whew! They're worse than puppies! What am I going to do with them?"

Thinking of puppies gave Sam an idea. "If you can train dogs, why not dinosaurs?"

"Brilliant!" said Mr. Puff. "And then maybe you'd like one as a pet. They're very sweet."

"Thank you," Sam said, "but I'd rather just visit them sometimes. I think I prefer my dinosaurs in books!"

Sam never told anyone
about the dinosaurs next door
– or his narrow escape.

But whenever he saw
Mr. Puff's cat, he always
took out a saucer of milk
to thank her.

Try these other books in
Series One:

The Burglar's Breakfast: Alfie Briggs is a burglar. After a hard night of thieving, he likes to go home to a tasty meal. But one day he gets back to discover someone has stolen his breakfast!

The Monster Gang: Starting a gang is a great idea. So is dressing up like monsters. But if everyone is in disguise, how do you know who's who?

Wizards: Here are three magical tales about three very different wizards. One is kind, one is clever and one knows more secret spells than the other two together.

Designed by
Maria Wheatley and
Katarina Dragoslavić

This edition first published in 2002 by Usborne Publishing Ltd.,
Usborne House, 83-85 Saffron Hill, London, EC1N 8RT, England.
www.usborne.com
Copyright © 2002, 1995, 1994 Usborne Publishing Ltd.

48